SHE'S IN THE ARMY NOW

The Story of One Female Army Recruit

ALICE V. BENNETT

Y Jones Publishing

Y Jones Publishing
Jacksonville, Fl.

Y Jones Publishing

SHE'S IN THE ARMY NOW

The Story of One Female Army Recruit

By: Alice V. Bennett

Published By: Y Jones Publishing
731 Duval Station Rd., Suite 107-143
Jacksonville, Fl. 32218
www.yjonespublishing.com

Cover Illustrations by: Shazeb Khan
ISBN: 979-8-9862627-3-4 (E-book)
ISBN: 979-8-9862627-4-1 (Paperback)
Copyrighted Library of Congress

Printed in United States
2 3 4 5 6 7 8 9 10
First Edition

She's in the Army Now does not discourage females from joining the military. The author thinks the military is a great tool for females to gain a trade which would not be available to them otherwise. A trade may be two to four years of college or a specific skill.

However, the military must protect female soldiers who enter the military from sexual trauma. Just as the military protects the country, the military must enforce rules and punish those that pose as threats to female soldier, and seaman from attacks.

CHAPTER 1

It was a lazy autumn morning in August 1973 when Joanne and her mother, Mama Rosa, were window-shopping at a small strip mall in Tampa, Florida. Neither of them had much money to spend, but they just enjoyed being out that day. Joanne had a three-year-old daughter named Cordelia who Mama Rosa was helping Joanne raise.

It was one of those days when the two women were reflecting on the past and worrying about the future.

Mama Rosa's husband, Mr. Mitchell, was the sole breadwinner of the family until he passed at the young age of fifty-four. Mr. Mitchell was a good husband and a good father who carried the needs of the entire family on his shoulders for about thirty years. He would not allow Mama Rosa to work because he believed that his children should have a parent at home at all times to ensure a proper upbringing. He was a Black barber who made a good living in those days when all men were expected to have a neat and well-groomed appearance. Yes, the Mitchell family was not rich, but they had a better-than-average home with plenty of food, nice clothes, almost-new cars, and things that most Black families only dreamed of having back in those days. Mr. Mitchell made sure his family was not in need. He was a good man and would not only give to his family, but he would give to other families who needed food or money to keep the lights on or to put food on the table.

He would cut the hair of the entire high school football team before games for free. He was a good man who loved his family, and his family loved him.

After his death, the Mitchell family put up a good appearance, but they were broke. No real money was coming in. Mr. Mitchell had life insurance policies, but the money did not last very long. The Mitchell family merged all of their resources that they could spare to make ends meet. Joanne's sister Brenda had gotten married only six months before Mr. Mitchell's death and did not have much to help her family. Joanne's younger sister, Margaret, was a junior in high school. Joanne had one brother named Charles who was in the US Navy and was married with two children. He helped the family as much as he could.

Mr. Mitchell had taught his family well; his motto was "If one has—all have." He taught his family to share and share alike. He also inspired in his three daughters the desire for independence and self-sufficiency to work. He told them that one day they would get married and should their husbands not treat them right, they would be able to take care of themselves. The family shared everything and made ends meet even though there was no money left to spend on fun and enjoyment.

One Friday afternoon while Mama Rosa and Joanne were walking enjoying each other's company, they came in front of an army recruiting center. Neither woman said anything, but they stared into the picture window. It was like ESP. Joanne said, "Do you think I should go in?" and Mama Rosa replied, "It would do no harm to just see what they have." They went in and that night Joanne was on a bus to Fort McClellan, Alabama, to United States Army basic training for women after taking placement tests. Cordelia, Joanne's daughter, stayed with Mama Rosa. Joanne was going to have a hard time leaving Cordelia. She thought of her beginnings.

Joanne was young when she went off to college. At the age of seventeen, she fell in love with the first guy she met at the freshman's welcome "meet and greet." He was a junior whose fraternity sponsored the freshmen meet and greet for the university. Joanne liked Henry a lot. He was conservatively dressed with a boyish face. He smiled at Joanne from across the room with the friendliest smile Joanne had ever seen. Joanne smiled back at the same time another girl started talking to her. Joanne had forgotten about the smile when she heard, "May I have this dance?" Joanne knew who it was before she turned and looked up and said a weak "Yes." They danced and talked the entire night. Henry was from a well-to-do family and had been trained how to behave when it came to the female sex. He was the perfect gentleman. Joanne liked Henry a lot.

The next day Henry called on Joanne at the freshman dorm. They sat in the day room and talked for hours. Henry was an honor student, president of the men's senate on campus, and president of the marching band. They got to know each other and soon became an item.

Henry and Joanne spent many a night cuddling and making out. Joanne was a virgin and had no intention of losing her flower. Henry respected Joanne for being a virgin. Most of their friends thought the couple were having sex every night. Henry would go through the motions of trying to get Joanne to give in, but when things seemed to be getting out of control, Henry would put a stop to it. Joanne's body would tingle every time Henry touched her. His kisses would leave Joanne wanting more. Henry had very strong lips from playing horns in the band. Joanne would melt in his arms from a kiss. It was very hard for Joanne to keep her virginity.

Henry and Joanne made it through her freshman year without sex. When they returned the next year, Joanne could not take it anymore. Henry and Joanne were at a friend's apartment, where they were playing around in the bedroom. Henry kissed Joanne and he could not stop. He kissed each breast and went down to Joanne's navel. He usually stopped at this point but this time he did not stop. His lips touched her womanhood and Joanne was on fire. Joanne wanted what she had never had. There was no stopping it now. Joanne got lost into Henry. Her body was consumed with passion. Joanne could not get enough. Their bodies merged as one. Hot, sweet sweat ran from their naked bodies, and they were lost in time.

The next day Henry voiced his disappointment with Joanne for having sex with him. He told Joanne she did not have any willpower because she let him have sex with her before they got married. She was dumbfounded. She loved him with all her heart.

Henry did not come to see her very much after they had sex. He only came when he wanted to have sex. Joanne had become a sex object to him.

Eventually, Joanne got pregnant. Joanne's parents made her come home. Henry was willing to marry Joanne under one condition. He wanted her to get a job and support them while he went to grad school at UCLA. Joanne's father told Joanne that she was his daughter and he was going to take care of her and the baby. He said if Henry mistreated her, there wouldn't be anyone nearby in California to help. Joanne was so happy she fell on the floor, and in that instant she fell out of love with Henry. Joanne made a promise to herself never to let her cookies go again until she was married. After Cordelia was born, Joanne was a proud mother. Joanne got a part-time job so she did not have to ask her dad for every penny she needed. Mama Rosa was happy to keep the baby while Joanne worked.

Mama Rosa loved Cordelia like her own child, so Joanne had not worried about her child when she joined the army.

CHAPTER 2

Joanne slept the entire trip on the bus filled with female army recruits. The ordeal of signing up, testing, and taking physicals at the enlistment center in Tampa, Florida, had taken its toll on Joanne both physically and mentally. Joanne had no idea of the time of night they arrived at Fort McClellan, Alabama. She woke up to a drill sergeant shouting out orders, "You greenhorns get the h*** off that bus and form a straight line." The line was marched to an old warehouse where nurses and other medical personnel checked teeth (like horses), checked reflexes, feet, and gave shots (who knows what kind) from one medical gun (no changing of needles or alcohol wipes. No cleaning from one recruit arm to another). The medical team asked stupid questions (checked their mental condition). Then the recruits waited until everyone was finished; the line marched to the supply room. Another sergeant shouted out questions about their sizes. Army green fatigues, T-shirts, army blouses and skirts, army dress greens, army boots, socks, and shoes were piled in the recruits' arms. Then they formed another line where bedding, blankets, and pillows were piled on top of the clothing. They were tired and hungry but no one said anything about food. The line moved to another empty warehouse room where everyone stood and listened to the rules of the army. The recruits were told they belonged to the United States Army and were property like a desk or a chair. They only had rights that the United States Army gave to them. They were also told that they were not to think, and the army was going to think for them, and all they had to do was follow orders and rules.

Joanne wondered what she had gotten herself into. It was too late to turn back now. She was tired, hungry, and sleepy when she realized she was in the army now. Sergeant Bell took the recruits to their new home in Company "A" barracks. Each recruit was assigned to a bunk bed in the barracks, and each recruit was also assigned one stand-up locker for hanging clothes and one footlocker for all other items.

The recruits changed from their civilian clothes and put on a pair of fatigues. This was the first and last time Joanne had on fatigues in basic training. It was around 3 in the morning. The GIs, no longer recruits, bagged all of their civilian clothes and took them into the basement for storage. At around 0330 hours (3:30 a.m.), the new GIs were led into the mess hall for sandwiches and drinks. After they ate, they went back to the barracks and finally went to bed. Joanne thought she was going to die from the lack of sleep. She had decided she would sleep forever. Besides, the next day was Saturday, and she could sleep in late. Even the open bay where everyone slept in one big open space did not bother her. Joanne had always had a bedroom to herself. Her father made sure their house had enough bedrooms so that each child had his or her own room.

It seemed as if Joanne had just laid her head on the pillow when she was awakened with the awful sound of the drill sergeant banging a stick against the wall lockers and shouting, get up you lazy #%^&*s. Joanne refused to let anything bother her sleep. She was tired to the bone. She turned over and went back to sleep. A few seconds later a pail of water came tumbling down on her head. Joanne jumped out of bed and was about to ask, "What the hell," when Sergeant Bell put her face inches from Joanne's face and asked, "How was your beauty sleep?" She yelled at Joanne to get that mess cleaned up. Sergeant Bell yelled out orders to everyone and left the barracks. The new GIs had thirty minutes to get the barracks cleaned for inspection, get dressed, then get in formation in front of the barracks to be inspected.

When Sergeant Bell came back, she walked up and down each row of GIs inspecting their uniforms. Sergeant Bell shouted her disapproval of the troop uniforms. She was in the faces of the new GIs yelling about how the uniforms looked like they had slept in them. One GI was put on KP (kitchen patrol) for having her hair too long and not pinned up. KP was used to punish the GIs. One was assigned to the kitchen to peel tons of potatoes, wash huge amounts of very large pots and pans, and clean the kitchen for the cooks. KP was a dirty and tiresome job. Sergeant Bell said that the GI's shoes looked like they were polished with Hershey bars. There wasn't anything the troops did that was right in Sergeant Bell's eyes. She never had a kind word and she shouted not talked to the soldiers. She also had more four letters words than the average sailor. Sergeant Bell got out on the wrong side of the bed every day. After inspection, they marched to the mess hall. Joanne had barely eaten some of her breakfast when Sergeant Bell ordered them back in formation outside. Joanne made a mental note to learn to eat without chewing.

Joanne was learning fast. She kept a low profile and never said anything to Sergeant Bell except "Yes, ma'am" or "No, ma'am." Joanne learned to "spit shine" her shoes by firing up a can of shoe polish with a cigarette lighter, pour the melted polish on the shoes, then buff until the polish went into the leather. Then she spat on the shoes, and then buffed to a high shine. Next, Joanne would iron her uniform while the others were asleep. Joanne only needed three to four hours of sleep unless she was dog tired; then she would sleep the whole day. The first day of boot camp she was dog tired. She learned to pace herself as much as possible after the water in the bed trick by Sergeant Bell.

Day two, the troop learned their daily routine. Joanne was shocked when she learned what was expected of the WAC troops. Joanne had pictured them in fatigues and army boots crawling on the ground in mud and climbing ropes with an M16 rifle over their shoulders and dog tags hanging from their necks. Joanne had it all figured out in her mind. The sergeant called for a five-minute break and all pulled out their packs of cigarettes from their rolled-up sleeves and lit up. Then they would march in union dressed in polished army boots while wearing army fatigues. Joanne had it all figured out.

Reality check—Company "A" 1st Platoon learned their daily routine. Out of bed at 0400 hours (4 a.m.), do toiletries, GI (clean) around their bunks, making sure the bunk bed blanket and sheets were so tight that a quarter would bounce off of them. At 0430 hours, the troop stood at attention at the foot of their bunk beds for inside inspection of dwelling. Everything had to be clean, including showers and latrines. The tiled floors must be polished to a high shine so Sergeant Bell could see herself in them. She would inspect each footlocker and if anything was out of place or folded wrong, she would destroy the contents. That person would be put on latrine duty for a week or KP. At 0450 hours the troop was lined in formation outside of the barracks. Sergeant Bell and some other sergeant would inspect each GI. This was when she loved to get into their face and yell about what was wrong with the GI's appearance as she inspected the uniforms. Not the fatigues Joanne had imagined, but the white blouse, light green skirt, folded-down bobby socks and black low-cut army shoes not boots. Even this uniform had to be exact. The collar had to be starched and pointed in the correct direction. After inspection they marched around the fort, singing cadet songs like, "We are army, mighty, mighty army, and wherever we go they will know, we are army, mighty, mighty army, one, two, three, four." Another marching song was "Ninety-nine bottles of beer on the wall, take one down, pass it around, ninety-eight bottles of beer on the wall …". At 0600 hours they marched to the mess hall for breakfast.

After breakfast, the troop would get back into formation and march to "building 8." Joanne's imagination went wild again. She was sure "building 8" housed an indoor shooting range or somewhere to train to defend our United States of America. Joanne could not believe what "building 8" housed. Did she not join the United States Army to live on the edge and learn a marketable trade?

"Building 8" housed Revlon makeup classes. Yes, Revlon cosmetic classes. Each GI had her own station with every makeup one could imagine. There were about eight instructors from the Revlon Corp. to teach the troop how to apply makeup and other grooming things. Makeup class lasted four hours daily. Joanne learned how to line the eyes, how to shade the cheeks to narrow the face, how to apply lipstick to make you look smart, and how not to put on lipstick to make you look like a whore or streetwalker. After the Revlon classes, the troop marched back to the barracks to rest and change into shorts the same color as the skirts. They changed their black army shoes for white tennis shoes. They marched double-time to the gym after changing for physical training. PT consists of modified setups, pushups, running in place, and a daily run around the inside of the gym.

The only thing that Joanne did in basic training that resembled the US Army was going into a gas chamber. One Saturday morning Sergeant Bell came to the barracks and yelled to be in formation by 1100 hours. Sergeant Bell marched the troop to several tents in the woods. There were other NCOs (non-commissioned officers) there also. Twenty soldiers were called into one of the smaller tents at a time. When Joanne's group was called into the tent, she was shocked to learn they had to go into the gas chamber. Inside the smaller tent, Joanne was issued a gas mask named "Oscar." They were taught how to use Oscar and how to put it on and how to seal it so no gas could enter the mask. After, the sergeant instructed the GIs in the small tent on what was expected of them in order to pass the test. If they failed, the whole process would have to be repeated. Twenty GIs would enter the large tent at a time. They would not wear their Oscars. They had to enter the gas chamber and sit on any bench. After a minute someone yelled,

"Gas." Everyone had to hold their breath, take out their Oscar, put it on and seal it. Joanne's eyes and skin were burning, and her lungs felt like they were going to explode from holding her breath. If the Oscar was not sealed properly, the gas would get into the eyes, mouth, nose, and lungs, which was very painful. Joanne had to sit for another five minutes until someone called time. Joanne ran to a barrow that had water in it and washed her eyes and face. Joanne's red eyes and skin burned for the rest of that day.

This was the Women's Army Corp (WAC) basic training for eight weeks, August 1973. Joanne made it through basic training after passing her makeup tests (put on makeup and style hair), and PT tests (sets of pushups, sets of setups, and two laps around the gym). All exams had a time period to finish. Everyone in Joanne's troop made it through basic training except two GIs. They were recycled (repeated basic training).

Joanne met a lot of women from all over the country at basic training. They became sisters in arms. They exchanged addresses and phone numbers and vowed to keep in touch. Joanne would never hear from any one of these women ever again. It was time to move on to the next adventure. Basic training was over, what a joke!

CHAPTER 3

After basic training, Joanne went to AIT (advanced individual training) at Fort Dix, New Jersey. Joanne was assigned to Company "A" training barracks, better known as the trainees' WAC shack. At AIT, soldiers (males and females) go to schools to learn their future job skills. The skills are coded and are called MOS (military occupation specialties).

Joanne joined the army with a guaranteed MOS to work in the computer field as a computer specialist. She was so excited to finally get her hands on mainframe computers. The excitement was shorted-lived. Joanne learned that her recruiter in Tampa made a mistake and guaranteed Joanne a MOS that the army did not have at Fort Dix. In others words, Joanne was guaranteed a MOS that did not exist.

Joanne stayed in limbo at the WAC shack for almost a month with nothing to do, while the army was trying to figure out what to do with her. Unlike basic training, AIT did not have many restrictions. The soldiers were free to go as they pleased whenever they did not have duty, classes or barracks restrictions. Joanne spent most of her days at the PX (post exchange) or walking around the main post.

Joanne was a friendly person who trusted almost everybody. She loved meeting new people. One day Joanne was trying to pass the time when she went to the post exchange. She was leaving the exchange and walking back to the barracks when a tall, dark-skinned soldier with pearly white teeth approached her. Although Joanne's father was tall and lighted-skinned, the man reminded Joanne of her father. He had a beautiful smile. He talked to Joanne about the weather and wanted to know how she liked Fort Dix. He said he was from New Orleans and he had just returned from Vietnam, and he was a heavy-duty truck driver for the army. He asked if he could take her to the movies that night. Joanne wasn't sure and hesitated when he said he knew her barracks sergeant. He said that he was going to call her and let her vouch for him. Joanne went back to the barracks when Sergeant Stewart came to her and said Jim was a decent guy and she was going to arrange for her to go to the movies that night with him. Sergeant Stewart told Joanne she was restricting the rest of the barracks for general cleaning (GI the barracks).

Joanne thought this was her lucky day. She had met someone and didn't have to clean the barracks. Jim came to the barracks at 1900 hours (7 p.m.). Sergeant Stewart called Joanne to the office. Joanne saw Jim and Sergeant Stewart talking when she entered the room, but thought nothing of it. When Sergeant Stewart saw Joanne she hurried and left the room but not before she said, "Have a good time," and winked at Jim.

Jim led Joanne to the car. He opened the car door for Joanne like a gentleman. He did not talk. Joanne sat next to him and tried to start a conversation. Jim seemed like a different person from the friendly soldier she had met earlier that day. Joanne's sixth sense started to set in. She was regretting her decision to go out with this unknown man. Joanne gave up trying to talk to this person. She saw the theater come into view. She opened her mouth to tell him he was passing it, when he reached over and slapped her and told her to be quiet or else. Joanne knew she was in trouble. She did as he said hoping this was all a joke. In her mind something bad was going to happen and she did not know how to get out of it. Joanne reached for the door handle, when he hit her again. Joanne had never been in a situation like this before. She did not know how to defend and protect herself. Joanne went into survivor mode. She decided to keep quiet and look for a way out. Her heart was beating so fast, she thought she was going to have a heart attack.

After driving for over twenty minutes, Jim stopped the car and told Joanne she could scream if she wanted to because no one was going to hear her. Joanne tried to see where she was but it was too dark. Joanne wanted to scream for help, but her sixth sense told her that was a sure way to be killed.

Jim hit Joanne in the face with his closed fist and told her to get in the back seat. Joanne saw stars and white flashes. She was in a daze. Jim hit Joanne again and said in the ugliest voice to get into the back seat. Joanne could not think, she opened the door to the front seat and got into the back seat. Joanne sat very still in a twilight daze wondering what he was going to do to her. She had seen movies where a killer loved to kill for enjoyment. Joanne's heartbeat was racing and the cool night air felt as if it was not going into her lungs. Joanne thought she was going to have a heart attack.

It seemed like hours instead of seconds, since Jim opened the other back door and got into the back seat. With one movement, Jim grabbed both of Joanne's legs and pulled her onto the back seat horizontally. He quickly went under her dress and snatched her panties off, hurting Joanne in the process. Joanne knew she was going to be raped. She started to mumble, "No, no, no," when Jim hit her with his fist and told her to shut up. Without any fanfare, Jim thrust his full manhood deep into Joanne's dry vagina producing screams out of Joanne. Jim told Joanne to shut up or he would kill her. Through all the pain, Joanne willed herself to be silent and tried to think of how to save her life. Jim plunged harder and harder over and over again until

Joanne became wet. Joanne felt as if he was trying to tear her apart. It seemed like hours had passed, when Jim grunted and came in Joanne. He lay on top of Joanne until he recovered his breath. Joanne was glad it was all over and she was still alive.

It was not all over; Jim did unthinkable other things to Joanne that she is still trying to forget. He used his fist anytime Joanne tried to stop him. Jim would hit Joanne in the side of her face with his fist so hard, Joanne saw stars of white, red, and blue. Joanne thought Jim had broken her jaw because the pain was so great. Each time Jim's manhood got hard again, he would get back on Joanne and bang his penis into her brain. Whenever Joanne did not move her body, he would use his fist in Joanne's jaw and say, "Move your body, bitch." Joanne did as she was told through the horrible pain and fear. Time did not have meaning. Joanne did not know if she was there two hours or eight hours. She was in hell. There wasn't a part of Joanne's body that Jim did not abuse. He twisted her body in positions a gymnast would have had a problem performing.

By the last time Jim got on top of Joanne, she was ready to die rather than endure another second of his rage. Finally, Jim had his fill and just stared at Joanne. Joanne cried in silence while the hot tears rolled down her face stinging the broken wounds on her face, and she knew he was going to kill her. He was a soldier in the United States

Army and was not planning to end his thirteen-year career because of rape. Jim was going to kill the only living person who could end it all for him. Jim wrapped his hands around Joanne's neck like he was going to massage it, moving them up and down. Joanne knew it was time to die. He tightened his hands slowly around her neck when Joanne's hot tears fell on his hands. He eased his hands and stared into Joanne's eyes.

Joanne had a guardian angel protecting her. It had to be an angel who told Joanne to be very silent although she was in great pain and scared to death. It had to be an angel who told her just to sit still in her torn-up clothes with her round breasts and female privates uncovered not to make a sound when Jim started talking. Jim told Joanne he should kill her and leave her body in the woods. It had to be an angel who told her to hold herself together. Jim stared at Joanne for about five minutes more with his hands still around her neck; when he finally spoke, he said he was going to let her go. He told Joanne that if she told anyone, he was going to find her and kill her like he did the others. Joanne knew he was telling the truth.

Jim drove Joanne back to the main part of Fort Dix where he unceremoniously put her out on a corner. It had to be after midnight because there were few cars on the road. Joanne's clothes were torn, her face was bloody and swollen, she had no shoes on, she had a hard time walking because her private parts were swollen and torn, and no one in any of the few cars on the road stopped to help her. She tried to cover herself up with what was left of her clothes as she walked back to the barracks as best as she could.

As soon as Joanne entered the barracks, the night-duty trainees ran to help her. Someone went and got Sergeant Stewart. Sergeant Stewart took one look at Joanne and mumbled, "That bastard." She took Joanne to her private quarters and treated some of the wounds on Joanne's face and bite wounds on Joanne's bloody nipples. Later Stewart put ice packs on Joanne's swollen face and breasts. She then helped Joanne to the showers and had someone stay with Joanne while she went for clean clothes. She brought back clean clothes and two disposable douche washes. Joanne started to question Sergeant Stewart about the douche but she wanted to wash all of Jim from her body. Joanne used the douche although it burned her raw flesh. But she found the douche did not wash all traces of Jim from her body. She could still smell and feel him inside of her. Joanne scrubbed her skin until it was raw. She stayed in the shower so long, Sergeant Stewart had to make Joanne come out. Sergeant Stewart also disposed of the torn-up clothes for Joanne. When Joanne looked into a mirror, she did not recognize herself. She had black eyes, a swollen jaw, cuts, and red hand marks around her neck. She did not look at the rest of her body. It was too much for Joanne.

CHAPTER 4

Sergeant Stewart told Joanne how sorry she was for what had happened to her. She told Joanne not to worry, she was going to take care of him and not to be afraid. He was not going to bother or hurt her ever again. She also warned Joanne about filing rape charges while in the military. She told Joanne to leave everything to her; she was going to take care of everything. Sergeant Stewart explained how the female is always to blame and it was best not to file charges. For example, she told Joanne how Private Woods (another trainee in AIT) was going to get a dishonorable discharge because she reported being raped, and the army said she lied. Joanne and most of the barracks' privates thought Private Woods was mentally stressed, but did not know the reason she was mentally unbalanced. Rumors were Private Woods was crazy. Joanne felt sorry for Private Woods now that she knew Woods had been raped. Sergeant Stewart made sure Joanne understood that she was supposed to keep silent about being raped. Joanne did not know what to do with Jim threatening to kill her and Sergeant Stewart warning her she would be shamed and discharged from the army if she reported it. Joanne didn't want to go home in shame, but did not want to stay at Fort Dix.

Sergeant Stewart let Joanne sleep in her quarters that night. Joanne cried out several times during a dream of Jim raping and killing her. Joanne was grateful for Sergeant Stewart's help. During the night Joanne had vaginal bleeding and Sergeant Stewart took her to the Walson Army Hospital's emergency room. Sergeant Stewart talked in private with the military ER nurse. The nurse checked Joanne herself never calling in a doctor; she gave Joanne some pills to take every eight hours for ten days. When Sergeant Stewart left the room, the nurse gave Joanne a sheet of paper and told her to hold on to it and tell no one about it, not even Sergeant Stewart. Sergeant Stewart took Joanne back to her quarters where Joanne stayed for the next three days. Joanne stayed in bed but did not get much sleep. Sergeant Stewart gave her pills the second night to help Joanne sleep, but Jim still came in her dreams.

Over the next weeks, Joanne's body was healing, but her mental wounds were getting worse. Joanne trusted no one. Joanne could not sleep much and when she did sleep, Joanne would wake up in a sweat. She had nightmares of Jim raping her and she would wake up thinking Jim was killing her. The dream would stay with Joanne the rest of her life. Joanne went over her actions and wondered what she did to make a person treat her worse than a dog. Sergeant Stewart helped Joanne clean her area and even helped her wash her clothes. She would order food to the barracks for Joanne since Joanne did not like to go outside to the mess hall.

One day Joanne wanted to go to Morristown Mall to buy a gift to send to Cordelia; Sergeant Stewart quickly volunteered to take her. While driving from the barracks, Sergeant Stewart said, "He's gone." Joanne was instantly alert. She asked, "Who's gone?" Sergeant Stewart said Jim was transferred to Germany. Joanne was glad but wondered if this could be a joke on her. How could she trust anyone? The last few blocks of Fort Dix were the housing areas. When Stewart and Joanne were passing an enlisted housing area, Joanne said when she became permanent party (out of training status), she was going to get base housing and send for her daughter. What Sergeant Stewart said next alerted Joanne of trouble again. Sergeant Stewart said, "You'll get housing and you'll be the mommy and I'll be the daddy." Joanne's internal alarm went off screaming "danger, danger." Joanne kept silent because she did not know what to say.

Joanne trusted no one. Now Joanne sometimes left the barracks, but talked to no one. She went to very public places but did not even return a good morning or good evening. She tried to stay far away from Sergeant Stewart. Stewart was finding excuses to ask Joanne to come to her quarters. Stewart was regularly ordering pizzas and other food and inviting Joanne to eat with her.

Joanne, mentally damaged, had to protect herself the best she could. When a bad boy type named Joseph Lane tried to talk to her, she ran like a child. Another private told Joanne that Joseph was trouble but a lot of girls wanted to date him. He was bad and other male GIs did not bother him. He pretty much did what he wanted. When he hounded Joanne for a date, Joanne said no. However, Sergeant Stewart saw Joanne talking to Joseph one day and she went into a rage. She told Joanne she was asking for trouble and demanded Joanne leave Joseph alone. Sergeant Stewart nearly ordering Joanne not to talk to him, made Joanne act faster than she planned. She was afraid of Stewart. She was as much a threat as Jim.

Joanne started putting two and two together. To this day Joanne wondered did Sergeant Stewart set her up to be raped by Jim? She did know a lot about him. Did he rape Joanne and then turn Joanne over to Sergeant Stewart? Was she counting on Joanne hating men after the rape? Did this occur before with other trainees? Regardless, Joanne was not letting herself be raped again by a male or female.

Joanne weighed her options, date a bad boy to keep her safe or duck and hide from seedy people like Sergeant Stewart and Jim. Joanne chose Joseph.

CHAPTER 5

Joseph wasn't a gentleman, but he treated Joanne with respect in his unconventional ways. He was adopted and raised in a Catholic church by nuns in New York City. Joseph's mother left him on the steps of the Catholic church at six months of age. He stayed there until he finished high school at age eighteen. After leaving the orphanage he bummed around for a year or two until he got into trouble with the law. A judge ordered Joseph to jail or he could go into the military.

Joseph became a major part of Joanne's life at Fort Dix. Joanne did not date anyone else. Other guys would not hit on Joanne because she belonged to Joseph. Joseph was loved by almost everyone. He was the go-to person for everything. He had a strong voice that would melt anyone's heart. When he was in the orphanage, he said the nuns would hit their knuckles with a stick if they mispronounced a word.

Joseph was an expert in sex. He told Joanne he had his first sexual experience at the age of eight at the orphanage. He said when the nuns went to pray and sleep, they would mate up. Age was just a thing. He said he had sex at eight years old with a sixteen-year-old girl who taught him the basics. Joseph told Joanne it was another orphan, a seventeen-year-old girl, who taught him the advanced sex moves.

Joanne did not tell Joseph what had happened to her, but he knew something was wrong with Joanne. He took his time and slowly introduced sex into their relationship. He was gentle at first, but Joanne was still withdrawn from him. Joseph talked Joanne into smoking marijuana to calm her nerves. It became a ritual; Joanne could not have sex without a mind-altering drug. The sex was the best Joanne would ever have. Joseph knew all the tricks and he had the body to use them. He was tall, slim and had just the right amount of muscles. Joseph played with Joanne's sexuality. He was such an expert; he could bring Joanne almost to the top of the mountain and then make her climb it again and again until Joanne would explode. Joseph did not give Joanne a lot of drugs, but just enough so Joanne would let go of her ghosts for a short time. Sometimes Joseph would get Joanne high so they could explore each other's bodies without sex. They would just touch and caress each other's bodies. Joseph said he was teaching Joanne how to love her beautiful body. Joseph knew Joanne could not deal with sex without the drugs.

Sergeant Stewart was still coming after Joanne. She probably could have killed Joseph. She would call Joanne for help with putting up curtains in her quarters, or she had ordered a pizza and it was too big for one. She used any excuse to talk to Joanne. Joanne wanted no part of Sergeant Stewart. Joanne was positive that Sergeant Stewart set her up with Jim to be raped. She was actually afraid of her.

Joanne's angel was still with her. Joanne was detailed to base personnel in the nick of time. At that time, the army was changing personnel systems from BASOP to SIDPER. Each soldier in the First Army's (which was hundreds of thousands) personnel records had to be keyed into cards for the computer one at a time. Joanne knew how to keypunch from her civilian jobs, and was very good at it. After one day of sealing envelopes on detail, Joanne let the personnel warrant officer know she was a trained keypunch operator. The warrant officer put Joanne on the data entry team. After seeing her work, the warrant officer immediately contacted the Pentagon and had Joanne assigned as a permanent party at Fort Dix.

Being assigned to Fort Dix made Joanne eligible to apply for base housing. Joanne went to request an apartment for Cordelia and herself. She was shocked when the person over at housing told her she needed to marry a real soldier to get base housing. Joanne tried to tell him she was a soldier. The man laughed and said come back after you marry a male soldier. That was it; Joanne was stronger and meaner now. She called base headquarters and spoke to a General Bradley. She told him what the housing officer had said. General Bradley was infuriated, and put Joanne on hold while he made a phone call. He came back on the line and told Joanne to go back to the housing office and call him back after she'd talked to the housing officer. When Joanne walked into the housing department, the civilian housing officer met her at the door. He had a townhouse unit ready for her that day. He asked did she have furniture, and Joanne said no. The manager took her into another building full of odds and ends furniture and told Joanne to pick what she needed. Joanne picked a living room set, dining room set, queen bedroom group, and a twin bedroom set. He took her to another room where she got all the kitchenware and linens she needed. Just like that, Joanne was the first single female soldier on Fort Dix with base housing solely on her own merit.

Joanne sent for Cordelia and they had a real family there. It was Joanne, Cordelia, and Joseph. Joseph became a major part of Joanne's life at Fort Dix. Joseph was Joanne's protector. It was strange because other women would ask Joseph what he saw in Joanne, and Joseph would laugh and say there's nothing like a Florida girl.

Joanne stayed at Fort Dix for over eighteen months, and personnel counted on her for her know-how and speed of getting the work done correctly. After two days in personnel, Joanne talked the sergeant into changes to the data entry system, letting her reorganize the way they were doing things. In one month's time, production had risen 500 percent. Joanne's new organization and work were so good, Joanne's sergeant received a grade increase. Joanne received nothing. Joanne started thinking about her goals after a year of doing the same job with no advancement; she wanted to get away from Fort Dix. So, Joanne put in several requests to attend computer operation and programming school. Fort Dix did not want to hear about transferring Joanne. They had a good thing going with Joanne's work. They were getting too much praise from the Pentagon on the data creation from BASOP to SIDPER.

Joseph received orders to Germany. Joanne was losing her protector. Joanne put in a request for computer school a third time, which was denied. Joanne decided to go to the Pentagon herself and asked for the computer school after talking to Major Albert from Florida. In fact, the major drove Joanne to Washington, DC, to the Pentagon to see a sergeant friend of his. Joanne talked to the sergeant and he felt sorry for Joanne. He said their records showed that Fort Dix's commander general had been blocking her previous requests for computer school. He granted Joanne's request and told her not to say anything about it until she received her orders in two weeks. He explained that if word got out, Fort Dix could have the orders revoked. He said once she had the orders in her hand, Fort Dix could not stop them.

With orders in hand, Joanne let her duty station know she was leaving in one month. As Joanne expected, moves were made to get the orders rescinded, but it was too late for that.

Joanne moved out of base housing, sent Cordelia back to Florida, and moved back into the barracks for her last month at Fort Dix. The last month at work was awful. Everyone treated Joanne like a traitor. Joanne did not mind, she went into the military to improve herself, not only to fulfill the needs of the army. Her replacement came two weeks before Joanne left. She was all talk and no talent. Joanne knew the personnel department was in trouble the first time she met her. Her rank was staff sergeant and she loved to brag about what she knew and how she was going to run things. She even told Joanne that she wasn't going anywhere because Joanne's orders were being revoked. She also told Joanne that she was going to work under her. Joanne could not wait until she was alone to call the sergeant at the Pentagon. The sergeant told Joanne that as long as she had orders, she could leave. However, to be on the safe side, he told her to put in for leave for the remaining weeks and not to report back to Fort Dix. After the leave Joanne reported to her new duty station at Fort Benjamin, Indiana, never to return to Fort Dix, New Jersey.

CHAPTER 6

Joanne made private first class (PFC) at Fort Dix when she was assigned to personnel. When she reported to Fort Benjamin to computer school, she was the senior student in the trainee barracks. She was assigned acting sergeant over her female barracks of privates straight out of boot camp. The barracks were World War I open-bay barracks with two rooms in the back for the sergeant quarters. Joanne was in a new environment and felt like a weight had been lifted from her shoulders. She tried not to think about Fort Dix and the evilness there. Joanne did not smoke drugs anymore and tried to get back on track with her goals. She did not need protection anymore. She did not date. She had one goal: learn a new trade to convert to civilian life so she could earn an above-average living.

Joanne went to the first class, which was huge. There were about seventy people in one class. The instructor told the class that by the end of the last week of class there wouldn't be more than five people left. Each week the class was to be tested and only the ones who passed could continue. He also said that out of the twenty females in the class, he would be surprised if there was one left at the end. Joanne made her mind up that she was going to be that one female who finished the course.

All of the training barracks were under First Sergeant Willis. Sergeant Willis would tell Joanne when there was an inspection and tell Joanne she needed to restrict the girls for GI'ing the barracks. He would come back and tell Joanne to let two of the girls go out. Joanne did not know what to do. She knew what it meant. Joanne talked to the two privates and asked them if they knew what they were doing. Each said yes, so Joanne left it alone and excused them from duty. Each week they would go out after the first sergeant told Joanne not to restrict them.

Joanne did not like playing nursemaid to the young, silly girls. One private needed advice about her boyfriend at home. She was sending all of her pay to him, but he would not answer her phone calls or letters. Joanne told her she would meet someone who cares about her one day and stop sending her money to him. Joanne only hoped the private stopped sending money. Joanne was only a couple of years older than the girls but she seemed more mature than them. Joanne had aged fifteen years in the last two years. Joanne had no innocence left in her. Jim and Sergeant Stewart had taken all of Joanne's youth and trust in human beings from her.

Joanne studied every night after she put the privates to bed and turned out the barracks' lights at midnight. She would go into her quarters and hit the books. Joanne did not like to sleep at night. She did not know when Jim would pop up in her dreams to rape and kill her. Joanne's sleep consisted of nods here and there. After one of those dreams, Joanne would look over her shoulder for days. She would try not to venture into public places. Jim seemed too real and her body could feel the aches and pain all over again.

On weekdays, she would hurry through morning inspection of the barracks so everyone could have time to prepare last-minute things for their classes. At night, she would do a more intense inspection of the barracks so the barracks would not get in too much disarray. She posted the cleaning assignment on the door of her quarters. She was surprised the girls followed her orders.

Joanne had gotten into a good routine when the last week of her class came. She could not believe it; she was first in her class. A Sergeant Johnson was one point below her. Not only did she make it to the end, she was first in the class of four males and herself. The instructor told Joanne she could not be first in the class. They had never had a female near the top of the class. The instructor took two points from Joanne's grade for holding something in her left hand. This had nothing to do with the class. Sergeant Johnson was first in the class and received a one-rank increase; again Joanne received nothing.

CHAPTER 7

When Joanne left Fort Ben Harrison, she went home on leave for thirty days. Joanne was glad to be home. Few people at home knew Joanne was in the military. Joanne liked it that way. Joanne was working in Georgia as far as anyone knew. Mama Rosa noticed a change in Joanne. She asked Joanne if everything was OK? Joanne seemed restless to Mama Rosa and a little bit nervous. Mama Rosa noticed Joanne did not sleep much and Joanne cried in her sleep sometimes. Mama Rosa could not get Joanne to talk about what was worrying her. Joanne told Mama Rosa it was going to Korea that bothered her. She had never been out of the country before. Joanne hoped Mama Rosa bought the lie. Mama Rosa did not completely believe Joanne, but she let it go.

Being home was like old times. Mama Rosa, Cordelia, and Joanne went on daily rides around town and enjoyed each other's company. They went to other well-to-do neighborhoods and daydreamed about how they would one day live. They went to new places to eat and went to the beaches. Joanne did not go out with her old friends. Mama Rosa asked Joanne why she had not seen her friends. Joanne only said she had outgrown them. Mama Rosa knew something was wrong, but she realized that Joanne was not going to tell her what it was. Joanne had changed; she was no longer the friendly, outgoing person who had left Tampa in 1973.

Joanne was a female on the edge ready to run if anyone said boo. Joanne knew what one human being was capable of doing to another human being. She now knew what a wolf in sheep's clothing meant. She had lived through the dark secrets of a lot of women. Jim aged Joanne, making her older than her twenty-two years of age. She felt like she was in her seventies. Her face and jawbones ached a lot from the beating from Jim. Her body ached all of the time, her face looked old and sad; she dressed old-fashioned so no one would notice her. She felt as if she was the ugliest person in the world. Joanne had lost all of her confidence. Without Joseph and his protection, Joanne felt herself slipping into darkness with Jim, the ruler of a deep dark hole … Joanne tried hard to give off a happy appearance to keep Mama Rosa from worrying about her. The month's leave went fast and Joanne was off to Seoul, Korea, her new duty station.

Joanne traveled on a commercial flight to Washington state where she boarded a Northwestern 747 jet to Tokyo, Japan. This was Joanne's first overseas experience. When the 747 got over international waters, everyone on the plane let their hair down. One of the flight attendants announced that the plane was over international waters and there were no limits on alcohol. Someone went into one of the bathrooms and stocked marijuana cigarettes on the washbasin. There was a stream of passengers who entered that bathroom one at a time. Even one of the pilots went in for around five minutes. Joanne enjoyed the flight to Japan. She met other military personnel and a lot of Koreans, Japanese, and other Americans. Joanne played cards for hours with unknown people. Joanne felt safe on the plane. People were drinking, singing and even dancing in the aisles. She was surprised to be at ease on the flight.

The army paid for two nights at the downtown Tokyo Hilton. They also paid for all meals at the Tokyo Hilton hotel in the heart of Tokyo, and gave $50 per day for spending money. Joanne checked into her American-style room. She turned down the offer from the desk clerk to try a Japanese-style room. One of the other female soldiers took a Japanese-style room and was surprised to find that there was no bed. She had a mat on the floor, and the wall between the rooms was sliding rice paper doors. After Joanne showered, she met some of the military females from the plane in the lobby. They went walking in very clean, beautiful streets. There were three African American and three White

American females. As they were walking, they spotted a Burger King to eat at. One of the girls looked back and noticed a crowd of Japanese people was following them. They stopped and tried to communicate with word phrases and enactment of the words. The people were friendly with lot of smiles and giggles. One of them spoke a little broken English. She said that they had never seen Black people before and asked to touch their skin. After the Americans said yes, hands were rubbing on Joanne's face. The Japanese were surprised that the color did not come off on their hands. The mostly young Japanese were also feeling the hair of the Blacks. Joanne felt hands pulling and twirling her hair. The crowd bowed and thanked them and led them to Burger King. The burgers were good, but they cost much more than in the USA, and they tasted different. The group hopped on a bus that was very clean. There were little doilies on the headrests. The bus had an attendant who catered to the needs of her passengers. Joanne wondered why the United States did not have such graceful things. Everyone was so courteous; she noted that she would like to live there one day. The bus took them to the inner-city part of Tokyo where there were beautiful Japanese bonsai and cherry trees, and large Buddha statues and centers. Everything was clean and the people were very nice and friendly but curious about the foreign people from America. The day went by fast. The group headed back to the hotel a little before sunset.

The girls met for dinner in the hotel's dining hall. Joanne had her first Indian curried shrimp. It was spicy and hot. Joanne fell in love with the dish and ate shrimp curry for the rest of her meals in Tokyo.

Later that night the girls went to a club that was recommended by the hotel staff. It was a nice club that was filled full with Japanese locals. Almost everyone was very neatly dressed in American blue jeans and the latest fad tops and shoes from America. Joanne and her party were the stars of the night. They danced with each other and a lot of the locals imitated their dance style. When they made up a new dance, everyone in the club copied them. It was very chic in Japan to dress and act like Americans in a nice way.

Joanne let her hair down and enjoyed herself for the first time in over two years. There weren't any threats and she felt completely safe. No, Joanne did not see anyone who acted like they were going to rape her. She felt sad when it was time to leave and fly on to Korea.

CHAPTER 8

The plane landed in Korea in the afternoon. When the stewardess opened the plane doors, Joanne smelled the air that reeked of human waste. It was everywhere. Joanne tried holding her breath, but when she couldn't hold it any longer, the smell entered her lungs and there was no place that had any clean air. Joanne was in Camp Mitchell where troops were processed into the country. She was told that they were to stay overnight. Camp Mitchell was a dirty, smelly place. The army cots were nasty-looking and Joanne decided she was not going to sleep on one. Tears filled Joanne's eyes as she wondered what she had gotten herself in for. The entire base in Korea surely did not look like this. Joanne thought she had seen it all when the biggest rat, the size of a large cat, ran across the floor in front of her. She and other females screamed and a little Korean man ran and caught the rat in his hands. He took it outside and body-slammed it several times to kill it. That was it; Joanne looked through her welcoming papers and found the phone number of her work assignment in Korea. She called them and they told her to stay put; they were on their way to pick her up.

Sergeant LaBlount of the United States Navy came to pick Joanne up from Camp Mitchell. He told Joanne that she was assigned to a top-secret joint service command. She and her new coworkers all stayed in a navy house barracks on an army base. Each person had their own room. There were twenty-two males and three females of mixed services: army, air force, and navy.

Joanne's alarm system went off until KB (Katie Bryant, one of the other females) told Joanne the guys did not know American women existed. Almost all of them have yobos (Korean women) who took care of all their needs.

Joanne got sick the first night in Korea and had to go to the hospital. She could not keep anything in her stomach. When she arrived at the hospital, she saw some of the fellow passengers there. A nurse talked to each one and gave them tiny white pills to take and sent them back to their barracks. Joanne later learned that almost everyone got sick when they first arrived in Korea. She was told that the Koreans save their human waste until it is picked up in the mornings. It was used to fertilize agricultural land. The bacteria from the waste was airborne and made new people in Korea sick until their immune systems got used to it.

Sergeant LaBlount introduced Joanne to the rest of her housemates. They seemed OK, but Joanne was going to keep her guard up. There was one bathroom with two stalls and one shower for the females, and one bathroom with eight stalls and five showers for the males. The female bath area was off-limits to the males. Each bedroom had a full-sized refrigerator and window air conditioner. The house had a Korean maid and housekeeper (Mr. and Mrs. Lee). Sergeant LaBlount was in charge of the house. If anyone had a problem they must go through the chain of command. Sergeant LaBlount (navy) was the first link, then Sergeant Major Henson (army) was second, Captain Bushy (air force) was third, and Captain Bings (navy) was the fourth and final link. The joint command unit had twenty-five enlisted people. The house had thirty rooms, so the navy placed three of their personnel into the house that had nothing to do with the unit.

The unit house in Yongsan was one hundred times better than Camp Mitchell. Joanne was going to endure this assignment. She was still having the dreams about Jim, but not as frequently as before. Joanne loved working with the top-secret mainframe computers. She put all of her energy and time into her job.

She met an air force female from another unit one day and they became friends. They scheduled tours to Hong Kong and other places. Joanne was disappointed that she couldn't go on cheap tours on Korean airlines with her new friend, Mildred, because her top-secret clearance forbade her from riding on foreign airlines. They went to Walker Hill Korea, one of the famous gambling casinos in the Far East. They had field tours in Southern South Korea. On weekends they would travel on Korean buses to the southern parts of Korea. The countryside was beautiful with mountains and the seaside. The Koreans would dry fish, oysters, and shrimp on the beach, and they lived in huts on the shore. It was like stepping back in time. The people were poor, but they were happy and friendly.

Joanne settled in Korea and was happy to be there. She loved working. Joanne would spend a lot of time in the day room at the barracks where she would look at the TV. The day TV was equipped to show American TV shows. A few of the other GIs would come in sometimes to watch shows. Everyone was friendly but rarely talked to each other. This was just fine with Joanne. She did not want anyone to get in her space and she surely did not want to get into theirs.

Joanne's work schedule varied because the computer system was up twenty-four hours, seven days a week. Sometimes Joanne went to work at 7 a.m. (0700 hours) and got off at 3 p.m. (1500 hours). Joanne would go to the barracks and to her room and change from her uniform to civilian clothes before she did anything else. The routine became a habit. Joanne was finally relaxing and enjoying her time in Korea. Joanne was promoted to E4 (spec 4, a lower sergeant rate).

One day Joanne got off from work, went to the barracks, and put her key in her room door. A hand went over Joanne's mouth and she was pushed into her room. She tried to fight this time, but she did not win. She tried to scream so Mr. Lee or Mrs. Lee would hear her, but no help came. It was Robert, the air force guy who was not a part of her unit. It was the guy who bought Korean females into the barracks late at night then beat them up. It was he who knew the Korean women would go to jail if he put them out because Korea had a curfew at midnight. It was him the evil one everyone in the barracks hated because of want he was doing to the Korean women when they would scream during the night, but they did not have the guts to report him.

Joanne thought, this could not be happening to her again. This evil, dirty monster was forcing her onto the bed with one hand still over her mouth. He used his legs, arms, and knees to pin her down on her own bed getting ready to rape her. The only words he said were, "Do you think you're too good for me, you stuck-up bitch? I am going to show you—always got your nose up in the air."

Joanne put up a fight as he struggled to get her panties off. Once he got them off, Joanne did not have a chance. He used his body weight to pin Joanne down while he used his free hand to enter Joanne's jewels. He used his own spit to lubricate Joanne. When Joanne's jewels were ready he entered her using his free hand to guide his manhood into Joanne while the other hand was over her mouth. After he was finished, he withdrew and came all over Joanne's stomach. He laughed, got up, straightened his clothes and walked out.

Joanne did not know what to do. Joanne knew the drill; she washed and reported it to the air force captain. Captain Hanley explained to Joanne how the unit was a joint top-secret command and they wanted to keep all their personnel together. If they made a report, the army would pull the army personnel from the unit and make them stay in army barracks. This would mean inspections, marching and PT every morning. He also put the guilt trip on Joanne by telling her that would not be fair to the good people in the unit.

Captain Hanley's solution was to assign a person in the barracks to protect Joanne. Again, nothing was done and Joanne had been raped again.

The old saying "out of sight, out of mind" was true for Joanne. After she was raped, she was put on the graveyard shift. She was moved to the end of the hall to a larger room. A Black air force guy called Doc Holiday was assigned to protect Joanne. Doc was a big guy with a gentle soul, who did not want to cheat on his wife with the free sex of Korean women. He did not want to carry the many diseases the other guys got from Korean partners back to his wife and family.

Joanne went into a deep depression after the second rape. She did not see her friend Mildred anymore. She stopped going on tours. Joanne did not go to the day room to watch TV anymore. Joanne went to work and back to her room. It may have been a blessing for Joanne to work the graveyard shift because she not only dreamed about Jim but now she started dreaming of Jim and Robert taking turns raping her. In her new dream, Jim begins killing her while Robert is standing over them laughing after they take turns raping her. Then Joanne would wake up in a sweat-drenched bed. Joanne walked around like a zombie. She did not care about anything anymore.

Doc Holiday would try to get Joanne to talk about her pent-up feelings. He did his best to try to ease Joanne's mind and comfort her. She did not tell him or anyone about Jim. The evil Robert was transferred back to the States. He probably raped others in the United States.

Joanne went to the mess hall to eat with Doc Holiday; he also made sure Joanne was safe in her room after work. Everyone in the barracks knew what had happened to Joanne, but everyone pretended that they knew nothing. Joanne felt eyes studying her when she passed by them. What were they looking for? Did they think a penis or something would be hanging between her legs? Did they think she would beg for someone to rape her again? Did they think she asked for it? Joanne was angry and depressed and wanted to ask, "What in the hell are you looking at?" However, Joanne said nothing. She just wanted to die.

Joanne stayed very low-key for the rest of her tour in Korea. When her time came to leave the country, the barracks gave her a going-away party. She stayed at the party for half an hour then went to her room until the next morning; then she traveled to Orson Air Force Base where she caught a flight to San Francisco, California.

Joanne flew back to the States on a military jet. She did not engage in small talk with any of the other passengers. She wanted to be left alone.

If Joanne wasn't so depressed, she would have had a big laugh about the military jet. The passengers' seats were all turned to the back of the plane. Flying backward for two thousand miles did not bother Joanne. When the plane landed, the other passengers were joyous to set foot on American soil. One soldier got on his hands and knees and kissed the ground. They got together and chartered a party bus to Las Vegas. Joanne was still depressed and declined to go; she took a cab from the air force base to the airport where she booked a flight to Tampa.

CHAPTER 9

Joanne was happy to be home where she was loved. Cordelia had grown and Mama Rosa had aged a little. The first few days home, Joanne stayed mostly in bed. She did not eat much and had few words to say. Even Cordelia noticed how unfriendly Joanne had become. Cordelia did not play with her mother like she used to. Joanne seemed mean to Cordelia and she was a little bit afraid of her. This was not the mother Mama Rosa had prepared Cordelia for. For over a month, Mama Rosa and Cordelia had been cleaning and buying all of Joanne's favorite foods. They were very excited to see Joanne and had planned all types of activities for the month of Joanne's leave. Joanne had earned one month's leave for pulling overseas duty. She was planning to spend the entire month in Tampa before reporting to her last duty station at Fort Gillem, Georgia, a small town outside of Atlanta, Georgia. Mama Rosa would sing old religious songs while cleaning the house. One day the radio was playing "The Rubberband Man" when Cordelia walked in on Mama Rosa dancing to the tune. Cordelia watched for a while then eased out of the room. Cordelia thought Mama Rosa was old, but Mama Rosa was only in her fifties. The fifties were old to the very young.

After the first week at home, Joanne got in touch with her old friend Irene. Irene and Joanne went to school together and became best friends. Joanne and Irene told each other their deep, dark secrets for years. Irene was a daughter of a school teacher and daughter of an alcoholic father. Other friends said Irene was born with fetal alcohol syndrome. Joanne needed someone to talk to. Joanne felt she could tell Irene everything that happened to her without Irene judging her. When Joanne called Irene, Irene had a problem remembering who she was. Irene said, "Joanne who? I don't know a Joanne." Joanne thought Irene was joking at first but soon figured out Irene wasn't herself. Joanne met Irene later that day and was shocked to see her looking so dish-washed out with large bags under her eyes. She was skin and bones, and could not remember one sentence she made. She kept repeating herself. Joanne asked Irene what had happened to her. Irene told her she got married to an older man with teenage and grown sons who lived with them. Irene repeatedly asked Joanne what her name was. They talked for a little while longer, hugged and said their goodbyes. When Joanne got home, she called Irene's mother. Ms. Solomon told Joanne that Irene married an alcoholic and she had become one too. Irene repeatedly refused Mrs. Solomon's help. She said she was glad that Joanne was home and maybe Joanne could get Irene to seek help for herself. Joanne tried to talk to Irene one more time but Irene did not want help. That was the last time Joanne talked to Irene. She died several months later.

After talking to other friends, Joanne learned that Irene's husband's sons pulled a train on her; they took turns raping her in their home. Irene had bad issues like Joanne and they could not confide their problems in each other. Maybe, if Joanne wasn't so focused on her own demons, she could have helped Irene.

Joanne spent the rest of her leave with Cordelia and Mama Rosa. They went to Orlando for a few days to see Disneyworld and other attractions. They had fun on picnics and trips to the local county zoo. Joanne enjoyed herself when they spent a few days at the beach. Joanne had finally relaxed a little when it was time for her to report to her new duty station. If AWOL wasn't a federal crime, Joanne would have stayed home with Mama Rosa and Cordelia and never returned to the military.

CHAPTER 10

Joanne reported to her unit at Fort McPherson in Atlanta, Georgia. There she learned she would be stationed at Fort Gillem, Georgia, located in Forest Park, Georgia, a little town southeast of the Atlanta metro area. Fort Gillem did not have living quarters so she had to stay in a motel until she rented an apartment. The army paid extra quarters allowance to help soldiers with rent.

Joanne was assigned to a high-level computer unit, which was fully staffed twenty-four hours, seven days a week. She was surprised to see KB (Katie Bryant) from Korea at her new duty unit. KB had a very outgoing personality. Everyone got along with her. Joanne was jealous of the carefree way KB handled things. Joanne knew her carefree days were over. Joanne knew she was damaged goods who had lost trust in others. She did not have the ability to get close to anyone. KB and the others soldiers tried to be friendly to Joanne, but she rejected their friendship.

Joanne found an apartment in Decatur, Georgia. She lived alone for a while. After several months she bought Cordelia to Georgia. She found a lady, Joan, who lived in her building to babysit Cordelia while she was at work. Joan was a single mom with two teenage girls. She and Joanne became good friends. Joan was married to her dream man when a nineteen-year-old took her husband. Joan was a bitter woman toward men. This made Joan and Joanne very compatible friends. Joanne did not want to have anything to do with men, and Joan thought all men were dogs.

Joanne and Joan went to clubs and concerts together. On the weekend, they would take the kids on outings to the zoo, parks, or Six Flags. They became bargain hunters together, going to flea markets and estate sales around metro Atlanta.

They both had issues and knew not to get in each other's business. Joanne and Joan became very close friends who respected each other's space, until Joan met Henry. Henry came to a convention in Atlanta from Arizona. They met in a department store in North Atlanta. He asked Joan for her opinion on a gift for his daughter's birthday. Joan guessed he was buying a gift for his wife. They talked and shared pictures of their children. Henry told Joan how he was trying to cope with losing his wife to cancer. They became long-distance friends. After a few months Henry did not do anything unless Joan approved it first. Joan was waking up each morning with a smile on her face. After six months, Henry came to Atlanta with a ring in hand. Joan did not plan a wedding; they went to the courthouse in Atlanta and became husband and wife. Joanne had to admit they were made for each other.

Joanne was happy for Joan, but Joanne did not have a babysitter after Joan moved to Arizona.

Metro Atlanta had some of the friendliest people in the world. Joanne went to a convenience store off Bouldercrest Road where she met Patricia Thomas.

Pat was married to her childhood sweetheart, Larry Thomas. They had two sons and one daughter. Pat was a friendly person and Joanne liked going to the store to talk to her. Since Pat worked at night, she offered to keep Cordelia with her kids while Joanne worked. Sometimes Pat's daughter would take care of Cordelia. Pat was a blessing to Joanne.

Pat loved to play bingo at the local centers around Atlanta. On some of Joanne's nights off from work, she would go with Pat to play bingo. Joanne did not really like to play, but she enjoyed being with Pat. Pat was a very colorful person who said whatever was on her mind no matter what.

Pat was not a cutesy person. She would do plumbing work on her house; she mowed the lawn, and did any other chore that was needed. Pat had a lazy husband who did nothing around the house. However, he had a good job and he took care of all the family's financial needs. Pat and Joanne became lifelong friends.

Everything was going well again until Joanne was put on night shift with Carlo McNeil. Sergeant Carlo was six years older than Joanne, married with four daughters. Joanne felt a little safe with Sergeant Carlo until he began to pry into her personal life. First he asked her whether she was married. Then he wanted to know her likes and dislikes. He told her stories about his children and home life. Joanne did not want to be friendly with anyone. She sure did not want to know about his family.

Carlo talked so much, Joanne started to relax around him. Carlo was just a husband who wanted to be friendly with his coworker. Joanne and PFC Jackson worked under Sergeant McNeil. Since two people had to be on the job at all times, Sergeant McNeil assigned Joanne to work with him three nights per week, Thursdays through Saturdays, and PFC Jackson to work with him Mondays through Wednesdays. On Sundays Joanne and PFC Jackson worked together.

Joanne soon found that Sergeant McNeil was not the faithful husband he tried so hard to project to Joanne. On Fridays and Saturdays nights, Sergeant McNeil started leaving Joanne in the big, old World War II hospital converted into a top-secret computer center alone all night. He would return before daybreak the next morning before the morning shift came in.

Joanne was afraid all the time in that ghostly building. She would hear water running and knocking between the walls; the sounds stopped at daybreak.

On one Thursday night, Joanne was at the console of the mainframe computer when an error occurred. Joanne went into the outer office to get Sergeant McNeil. They worked together to reboot the massive system and recover the very large amount of data on the system. They spent most of the night in recovery mode. When they finished, they went into the outer office to the control remote entry center and had coffee and snacks.

Joanne was sipping her coffee when she thought she saw "THE LOOK" in Sergeant McNeil's eyes. She told herself to stop, "There was not a wolf behind every bush." She continued enjoying her coffee in the cold room as Carlo talked about the computer system. Carlo passed the papers in his hands to Joanne when they touched each other. Their eyes met and they stared at each other for some seconds. Joanne quickly jerked her hands away and walked to the other side of the room.

Joanne had not felt anything like that since pre-army days. Joanne tried hard not to be near Carlo. Joanne was very surprised that she could be attracted to a man again. Joanne had to be on guard and never let that happen again. Not only was Carlo her boss, he was also married with children. Joanne was raised by churchgoing parents who taught her that she should never date a married man. Carlo made an effort not to have contact with Joanne. She was grateful for that. Soon, Carlo started leaving again every Thursday, Friday, and Saturday nights. He came in each night at the beginning of the shift, did his paperwork, spent the rest of the night out and came back before daybreak the next morning. Still, Joanne did not like being alone in the ghostly building, but it was better than being so close to McNeil.

Since Cordelia came to Atlanta, Joanne did not have as many dreams about Jim and Robert as before. However, since the encounter with Carlo, Jim and Robert invaded her sleep both day and night. Soon Joanne went back into a deep depression without much sleep. She tried to be a good mom and do her best at work. She loved Cordelia too much to let her suffer with her depression, so she took Cordelia back to Mama Rosa until she could get her head back in the right place.

Major Henderson, the executive officer for the unit, came to Joanne with papers for her to go TDY (temporary duty) to Keesler Air Force Base in Biloxi, Mississippi, for mandatory training. If a top-secret field was assigned, constant training was a must. Computer updates, software, and firmware changed often, and all personnel needed to go to the classes. KB had just returned from Keesler AFB the week before.

Biloxi, Mississippi, was a beautiful place in a quaint way off the Gulf Coast. The main street of Keesler AFB was a beach-lined street. It was the first time Joanne had seen a still-water beach without waves. On the East Coast, the beaches had beautiful waves; sometimes the waves were so large surfers all over the country would come to ride them.

Joanne reported to Muse Hall, a residential hall for TDY personnel where all the enlisted and junior officers stayed. It was a co-ed hall with two like genders to a room. There was a shared bath between each two rooms.

The dining hall had some of the best food Joanne had in the military. On one Friday, everyone went to eat when the word got out about whole lobsters for dinner. Not only did they have lobsters, they had all of the trimmings. To Joanne the meal was better than a five-star restaurant. Joanne put on about fifteen pounds during her two-week stay at Keesler. She did not miss one meal.

Joanne felt relaxed while she was TDY. She stayed away from all males as much as possible. Her dreams of Jim and Robert eased a little.

The two weeks went by fast and soon it was time to go back to Fort Gillem. Joanne dreaded the return to her duty station. She realized she had an attraction to a married man who was her boss. She made up her mind that she would wipe the feelings away.

The first day Joanne returned to Gillem, Major Henderson came by the duty station to ask Joanne how she liked Keesler. He said he liked to keep track of all of his people. He told Carlo he could take a break if he wanted to. Carlo jumped at the chance and went home for supper.

After Carlo left, the major talked to Joanne about the computer system. He talked about how to get ahead in the military. Then out of the blue the major asked Joanne if she had ever dated a White man.

A four-alarm fire went off in Joanne's head. Here we go again—Joanne thought she had a big bullseye on her back. Joanne did not answer right away. Her mind went into overdrive, thinking about what to do next. She backed up and started fumbling with the equipment, giving the appearance that she was very busy. The major stood there waiting for an answer. Joanne finally said no. The major started closing the gap between Joanne and him, then reached out and traced Joanne's lip with his index finger. Joanne had backed herself up against the wall. Joanne mumbled, "No, no," but the major was leaning his body against hers.

Joanne was so afraid; she knew what was coming next. Three was supposed to be the charm. Joanne's mind was racing; she knew she could not live if this happened again, even if she had to end her life herself.

She was praying, when they heard Carlo come back. Joanne was saved. The major jumped and said something to Carlo and left the building. Carlo looked at Joanne and asked if anything was wrong. Joanne told him no and went into the ladies' room and cried. She stayed in there for over an hour when Carlo came to the door and asked again if she was OK. She told him she did not feel well. Carlo told her to take the rest of the night off; he said if she still did not feel well the next day, she should call him in time so he could assign someone to take her place.

Joanne returned to work two nights later. She told no one about the major, not even Pat, her best friend. Joanne had already told Pat about Jim and Robert. Joanne was ashamed about it. She felt she caused things to happen to her. She must be a very bad and evil person.

Joanne continued to go to work; the major did not come back. Joanne knew it was just a matter of time until Major Henderson would make his move again. She had no plan to protect herself. She knew she had to stay as far away from the major as possible. When the major tried to rotate her to another shift, Carlo fought to keep her on his shift. Carlo liked that he could leave and the computer system was in safe hands. Joanne was good with computers. She preferred communicating with computers to people. She was very knowledgeable about computer languages. She loved that she could make them do what she wanted. Besides, computers did not rape people.

Carlo and Joanne became friends. They were used to each other. On one stormy Saturday night the electric power kept going out. Carlo had to stay the night because he had to go outside to switch power to the large and powerful generator. The computer had to be up and running at all times and the generator was powerful enough to run the whole building and computers. As soon as the power came back on the generator had to be powered down to reserve gas out of the large underground tank.

On one of the occasions when the power went off and the room was pitch-black, Carlo and Joanne ran into each other. Carlo put his arms around Joanne and held her. Joanne did not try to move. She felt safe like she was with Joseph. They just stood there in the dark like it was the most normal thing to do. After a while Joanne pulled back and Carlo picked up two flashlights, gave Joanne one, and then he went outside and turned on the generator.

Joanne and Carlo both acted as if nothing had happened for another week. They did not try to talk about it. Joanne made it a point not to get too close to Carlo and Carlo was doing the same.

A few months later, Carlo came to work looking depressed. He needed someone to talk to. Joanne was there with open ears. Joanne understood the need to talk to someone about their problems. She just could not talk to anyone about her own. Carlo said he and his wife were having problems. They had decided to get a divorce. He and his wife did not know how to tell their children. Joanne had figured that Carlo was seeing someone else all of those nights he left work, but she was shocked to learn that his wife was also seeing someone. Joanne suggested Carlo and his wife seek counseling and try to work it out.

A few weeks later, Carlo told Joanne his wife had filed for a divorce. He said he was not going to fight it because he believed that it was for the best.

Carlo started staying at work all night where he and Joanne talked about their life problems. Joanne and Carlo were truly friends. Joanne was glad to know she could have a male friend without feeling threatened. Joanne started enjoying going to work.

Joanne had forgotten about Major Henderson until the unit had a full office meeting on Saturday night at the NCO club on Fort Gillem. Everyone was there except two warrant officers who looked after the computer system during the meeting. Everyone was drinking at the meeting. Joanne was surprised about how much military personnel drank. Even at Fort Dix, office meetings normally took place at the local pub outside of the gates. In Korea, the base sold alcohol by the gallon.

After the meeting, everyone stayed and danced and drank a lot of alcohol. Joanne stayed close to Sergeant McNeil. Major Henderson came over to where Carlo, Joanne, KB, and others were standing and talking. He asked Joanne if he could have a word with her. Joanne's heart went to her throat. She could not get a word out of her mouth. The major leaned in and guided Joanne by the elbow from the group.

When they were out of hearing distance, the major asked Joanne if she had ever had a man perform oral sex on her. Joanne closed her eyes and stood there like a dummy. He said that was what he was thinking about doing to her the whole night at the meeting. He said he was going to tell Carlo to assign someone else to work the rest of the night in her place.

Joanne was so afraid and did not know how to get out of it. She finally told the major she and Carlo were dating. The major stared at her and walked away. He later went to Carlo and apologized for hitting on Joanne. He said if he had known, he would have never approached her.

Carlo did not know what the major was talking about, but he decided to go along with whatever Joanne had told him.

After the meeting, Joanne and Carlo had to go to work and relieve the replacements. Carlo asked Joanne what the major was talking about. Joanne broke down and told him everything the major had said. Carlo told Joanne she did well. He told her not to tell anyone any different. He told Joanne he was divorced and there was nothing anyone could say about them in a relationship. He assured her that he would protect her from the major.

Carlo was becoming Joanne's new protector like Joseph. The only difference was Carlo and Joanne were not sharing a bed, and Joanne did feel something for Carlo that she did not understand. Carlo did not take off anymore. He stayed every night with Joanne. They laughed and talked every night. Joanne was not afraid of Carlo and felt as if she had known him her entire life. Yet, Joanne could not tell Carlo about Jim or Robert.

One night Carlo bought two marijuana cigarettes to work. He stood outside the door to smoke one so the smell would not be in the top-secret building. Later, he asked Joanne whether she wanted to smoke with him. Joanne accepted the offer. They propped the door open and went outside and smoked the other marijuana cigarette. Joseph taught Joanne how to smoke and Joanne was used to smoking. But this time, Joanne felt different.

Carlo and Joanne went back inside the building and tried to work. They kept looking at each other as if they were seeing each other for the first time. It did not take long before they were peeling off each other's clothes. They had sex for the first time on the cold computer room floor.

Over the next month, Joanne could not get enough of Carlo. Carlo was around Joanne on duty and off duty. Carlo loved to smoke marijuana, so he did not notice Joanne only had sex with him when they got high. Carlo thought Joanne was special and never had a female who was into him, who would get high with him at any time.

Carlo asked Joanne to move in with him. They rented an apartment together. Carlo could not get enough sex with Joanne. He would look at her and want sex. Joanne enjoyed Carlo's lovemaking, but she always had a drink in her hands or on the nightstand if they did not smoke.

Joanne really loved Carlo, but she had demons named Jim and Robert. She could not share her demons with Carlo. She did everything she could to make Carlo hate her. It was too much for Joanne to love Carlo and keep her secrets.

Carlo felt hurt when Joanne would fight him off of her during the night. Carlo loved to sleep cuddled up to Joanne's back. Joanne would wake up fighting Jim who happened to be Carlo. She would say very mean things like, "Don't touch me" or "Stay on your side of the bed." Joanne felt sorry for Carlo, but she could not tell him that Jim and Robert were haunting her.

Joanne would be asleep and feel Carlo's legs on hers and see Jim raping her. Carlo should have guessed something was wrong. Joanne would be dripping with sweat and breathing at a rapid rate. She would get out of bed and go into another room to calm herself. Carlo took Joanne's actions as a rejection of him. Joanne always told Carlo to give her space. Carlo started hating Joanne because of her rejection. He never knew that Joanne loved him with all of her heart.

Joanne would ask Carlo to give her space. Joanne needed the space to self-protect her mentally. Joanne had made great progress as she fell in love with Carlo a man. She was trying to learn to make love without drugs. However, Jim and Robert were not going to let her.

Eventually, Carlo asked Joanne did she want him as her mate or did she only want a companion? Joanne loved Carlo, but she had to let him go. She could not stand letting him cope with her demons that she could not speak of. She told him she wanted a companion. That was the end of Carlo and Joanne. Carlo moved out to the barracks, then got orders to Germany.

Joanne was all alone once more. She had made up her mind that she would never have a mate of her own. She resigned herself to be a lonely woman with only Jim and Robert forever.

CHAPTER 11

Joanne got her honorable discharge from the army and went back to Tampa. She, Mama Rosa, and Cordelia were back together again. Joanne's two sisters and brother were married and lived elsewhere.

Joanne was happy to be with her family, but she was lonely, missing Carlo. Her heart felt broken and she wished Carlo and she were together. Joanne never thought she would find love again, but Carlo came into her life and almost completed Joanne.

Joanne felt as if she was cursed. Even when love came, she was being punished by Jim and Robert.

Mama Rosa and Cordelia went shopping one day and left Joanne home alone. Joanne was lying in her bed and thinking about how her life went so terribly wrong.

She wondered if she did anything to make Jim do what he did to her. Did she wear the wrong type of clothing, did she have the wrong facial expression, or did she have the wrong walk?

For the first time, Joanne tried to analyze how she got where she was. Did she not say no to Jim, Robert, and Major Henderson? What part of no do rapists not understand? If she had said, "Yes, yes," would they have stopped and not wanted her? Joanne wondered was she at fault? Was she at fault although she had Cordelia? Joanne was still innocent then. Cordelia's father was Joanne's first sexual partner.

Joanne was not in the habit of sleeping around with every Tom, Dick, or Harry. Joanne had never used drugs before. She did sip on one mixed drink each night she went to the clubs; otherwise, Joanne was not a drinker.

Joanne was digging deep into her core. Did she become pernicious with sex after the rapes because she wanted to, or had self-preservation dictated it?

She thought about Joseph; he was not the type of man she would have gone out with. Before the army, Joanne dated well-groomed men who had promising futures, respected the law, and came from good families. Joseph was an orphan from a bad part of New York City. He had no ambition before the court made him join the army. Yet, Joanne had developed a lot of respect for Joseph. He was a kind person in a rough way. Joseph would not rape a soul. Underneath the rough exterior was a good man who was not born to good parents. Joanne never heard from Joseph again. After twenty years she tried to locate him but failed.

Joanne thought about Carlo. She still loved him, but knew it was for the best that they parted ways. Joanne was not capable of giving love. She only could take love on her own terms. Carlo could never have understood the turmoil that Joanne was living with. He would never know the nightmares she lived through while they were together. Carlo would never know how much Joanne intentionally hurt him so he would be free of her. She wanted him to be happy. Joanne did not want to drag Carlo into the pit with her, Jim, and Robert.

Jim and Robert hurt Joanne so bad that the Major Henderson ordeal was a walk in the park. Carlo felt that Joanne was unsettled sometimes because of the major. Carlo almost guessed that Joanne was hiding something when he asked her who had hurt her.

Carlo met a lovely lady and they got married. As far as Joanne knew, Carlo was still happily married after twenty years.

Cordelia had grown up to be a lovely lady. Mama Rosa had passed away. Years have passed and Joanne still has nightmares about Jim and Robert. Joanne lives alone now.

She now has a special friend, Gerald, who loves her. He wants to marry Joanne, but she is not ready for him. She told Gerald the whole story. Gerald is an understanding man who wishes he could turn back the hands of time and take all the hurt from her. He is very gentle with Joanne. He has learned how to give Joanne space when she needs it.

Joanne loves Gerald also, but she is still dealing with Jim and Robert. Joanne knows Gerald would give her the world if she asked for it. Maybe one day Joanne will say yes to Gerald and live happily ever after.